SHINE BRIGHT

Nilma Shah

Clever Fox
PUBLISHING

Chennai • Bangalore

CLEVER FOX PUBLISHING
Chennai, India

Published by CLEVER FOX PUBLISHING 2021
Copyright © Nilma Shah 2021

All Rights Reserved.
ISBN: 978-93-94437-82-1

Be the light that shines bright always!

ACKNOWLEDGEMENT

Writing this book has brought me immense pleasure, joy and the opportunity to share what I've learnt.

I would like to thank my amazing husband for the support he has given me and my two undemanding children. I would like to thank my parents, too, for their immense support to get me to where I am.

Special thanks goes to my life coaches and mentors, Mitesh and Indu Khatri, as without them I would have never taken this bold step of writing a book.

To all my friends and family who have always supported me and believed in me, without you none of this would have been possible. A huge thank you.

To each and everyone one of you who have taken the time to read the book; a big thank you.

CONTENTS

INTRODUCTION

Each one of us has a unique and special purpose that lights our souls. As we grow up and experience life, we discover who we are and what we are meant to be. Unfortunately our paths are clouded, concealed or even cancelled by the complicated nature of the modern world. We become so lost and drowned in our negative emotions that we forget we have a purpose in our lives.

Are you happy doing the job you're in? Is it bringing you fulfillment? Are you paying only superficial attention to your most important relationships?

Wow, what an incredible journey it's been for me. Never had I thought that I would be able to write a book. But it has become possible, thanks to my coaches and mentors Mitesh Khatri and

Indu Khatri. As a young child I always dreamed of writing but that never materialised, due to distractions and inhibitions imparted by society.

I have always believed we are all born with a unique gift and the world is our oyster to explore it. We all get caught up with our routines and its frustrations that we tend to forget what we want, not what others want. This book explains how the little details we ignore in our daily life and routines can actually change our destiny and improve our lives overall. Our lives are balanced on four pillars, which are explained later in this book and if one falls, the whole temple shatters.

It is through our struggles and experiences that the universe speaks to us. It is up to us on how we perceive our situations; either as challenges or obstacles. As we begin to unfold all the layers within us, there is a whole new life waiting to be experienced by us. Our entire world shifts! We begin to accept ourselves for who we are and the people around us. We understand people's behaviour and will be more empathetic towards them.

Embrace the obstacles and learn from the lessons. Take in all the experiences and enjoy every moment.

DREAMS...FATE OR FREEDOM?

"Your entire life is a Virtual Reality, because you are seeing it only the way it happens in your mind.

—Sadhguru

We all believe we have a unique gift. Something that touches our soul deep down. Something that is going to make an impact on somebody's life or touch someone in a very special way. Each of us has a dream. At one time in our lives, we had a vision for the standard and quality of life we desire and deserve. But many of us no longer make the effort to achieve that dream, that vision because it is now clouded by our daily life routines and frustrations. My life journey has been to turn that dream into reality, to tap into that unlimited potential that lies dormant in each of us.

The day I decided to write this book impulsively is the day I realized that I'm living my dream. I'm extremely grateful to myself for recognizing and grabbing this opportunity, despite my fears. I feel incredibly humbled to share my insights and knowledge I have gained over the years that has shaped me. My travels and backpacking experiences have given me growth and wisdom.

Beethoven, the legendary musician, fought against all odds like deafness and depression to be able to do what his heart desired. He wanted to end his life after going essentially deaf, but his love and passion for art brought him back. He found a different way to keep following his dream, though he never performed in front of a large audience. He connected a metal rod to the piano and bit on the other end with his teeth to hear what he was creating. No obstacle or hurdle could stop him from pursuing his dream.

I believe everyone has the power to change at any moment and instant. There are resources within us that can turn our dreams into reality, just waiting for the day we decide to wake up and claim our rights. Deep inside you, there is a belief that the best is yet to come, despite you doing well or how challenged you may be. What is your true purpose in life? How are you going to realize your dream and potential?

The Japanese have a term "ikigai", which can be translated as "reason for being". This is a thing that gives a deep sense of purpose to a person's life and makes it worthwhile and gets you up in the morning.

Your true purpose lies beneath all the layers of past conditioning by the society and your own limiting beliefs and values. It's what ignites your soul, what brings you excitement, passion, awe and the contribution you have in other people's lives. Once you have discovered it, you have found your freedom.

My true purpose and my life's journey are building deep connections and adding value to all the people I have met in my life and going to meet in the future.

I have been searching for this, and found it through my own life experiences. In my career as an optometrist, I have come across many people from different cultural, social and economic backgrounds. Through this, I have learnt that people are not what their behaviour tells us to be. Each one of us is seeking a purpose. While some of us have found it, others have given up owing to the situations of their environment and the frustration caused by it. We all perceive the external world differently according to our past conditioning and beliefs. For example, two people attend the same event but will have different experiences based on their emotions.

What are you going to choose to focus on? Something you can have or something you can't have? We tend to focus on little things every day; our brain distorts, generalises or deletes the information. Are you going to focus on something you can control or something you can't control? Are you going to choose to focus on the past, present or future? We do all three, but if you're going to spend a huge portion of your time to enjoy the moment it's going to be the present and if you want to create a great life it's the future. There has to be a balance of both. What you focus on, flourishes. So choose wisely.

What meaning are you going to give to a particular situation? Is this the beginning or the end? Is this situation a gift from the universe or a punishment or a challenge? You're going to think, feel and act very differently when you're at the beginning of a relationship and when you're at the end of one.

What are you going to do? When you attach a meaning to a situation it gives you an emotion. If you think you're being punished in a situation, your emotions will be very different from taking the situation as a challenge. After graduating from university, I had secured a training job with great difficulty, located in a small town around 80 miles from London. As the travel distance was long from London, I had to move to the area. I rented an apartment which was a five minute walk to the workplace and that would save me the traveling time as I had to undertake exams at the end of the year. I still remember the first day I walked into the practice, very nervous and very apprehensive. Everyone was very welcoming and warm, until

I met my boss and mentor. He came across as very arrogant and unhelpful. Instantly, this took a toll on my self-confidence and I withdrew. As days passed, I settled more into the work environment, but it became more difficult for me to work with him. I felt hopeless and down. Also living on my own didn't help as there was no one to talk to. Eventually I took the exams and failed miserably. I then quit that job and moved to London where I found a better job. The working environment was much better. It made me feel comfortable and boosted my confidence too. My new boss was very warm and did everything he could to help me pass my exams, which I did with flying colors.

Had I approached the first job like a challenge rather than a punishment I would've passed my exams and had a better working relationship with my boss. I would have been happier and calmer and would have handled the work and exams better. I wouldn't have had to waste another year of training. It also taught me to be patient and never give up on what you really want.

You're not responsible for the situation you are in, but you are 100% responsible for the way you respond to it. Every day and every moment we are faced with decisions and choices that shape our destiny. It's what you do with those choices that will decide your future.

We all have resources within us that are either powerful or weak. These are not created by us, but a gift from the universe. These resources emerge in different ways. When we value something a lot, our power resources arise, and when we don't value something weak resources appear. What are you constantly thinking about? Are you giving it time, money, focus and space? To increase the value of something, you need to invest your time, money, focus and space in it and that will help you achieve your goals.

How can we create change that is permanent and lasting? At one point in our lives, we've experienced change that has made us feel disappointed and let down in the end. Why? This is because we unconsciously think of change as temporary and attempt it with dread and fear.

A good example of this is, a few years ago, I had set a goal that I wanted to eat healthily and have more energy throughout the day. I never seemed to achieve it because I never valued being healthy. My values never aligned with my goals. I never gave my health a priority and yet had a goal to be energetic. How did I turn this around?

I turned my 'should have' to 'must have'. I asked myself, do I really value being healthy? Is this a 'must have' for me? By asking myself this, I started thinking about it more and taking more action towards achieving the goal. I dedicated an hour a day to exercising and walking. It's what I enjoyed and I am passionate about. With time I started feeling better about myself, but less energetic. Why? My diet was below average. I would be exercising and not eating enough to make up for it. Eventually I turned my focus into eating more throughout the day and in 2 weeks found a difference. I changed what I demanded of myself and started believing that I could be a good and creative cook. I also changed my strategy, found a way to dedicate more time and effort in looking for new and exciting recipes.

Whenever you sincerely want to make a change, the first thing you must do is to raise the bar and act in accordance. Examples of people like Mahatma Gandhi, Abraham Lincoln, Leonardo da Vinci, Albert Einstein and many others, took a huge powerful step by raising their standards. The same is available to all of us if we have the courage to claim it. Once you have raised your standards, you must believe you can achieve them. If you don't believe it, you will be lacking the sense of certainty that allows you to reach your greatest potential deep within you. Our beliefs are like orders, telling us how things are, what is possible and what is impossible, what we can and cannot do. It is our beliefs that shape our actions, thoughts or feelings we experience. As a result, changing our belief system is vital to creating any real and permanent change. You must believe that we have already achieved our goals before we actually do. As a result you must take action and have a plan for it. The best way is to find a role model, someone who has already got the results you want and then tap into their knowledge. Learn what they're doing, what their beliefs are, and how they're thinking.

There are four areas in which our lives are balanced, like the wheels on a car. If one tyre is punctured or out of air the car would not move. Same goes with these areas. These are health, relationships, career and money. There could be the richest person on the planet, but he is still unfulfilled and miserable. His health is compromised and relationships are broken. We need a balance to have a fulfilled life. What are you going to focus on? What are you going to change?

CREATE YOUR DESTINY THROUGH YOUR DECISIONS!

What you seek is seeking you..
—Rumi

Decisions are made in every moment of our lives. Every decision that we make, be it positive or negative, our lives are defined by it and ultimately our destiny. Our decisions are made through the standards that we set for ourselves. Everything that has happened in your life that has either brought you joy or has challenged you is a result of the decisions you made. How are you going to live the next ten years of your life? What are you going to do differently today that will shape a better tomorrow?

This is the story of the movie *Me Before You,* which I watched recently and has resonated with me. It gives us an overview of how the power of decisions can impact our lives.

The sun is glaring through the window as she opens the curtains. "Good morning, sir. How are you feeling today?" Mark can barely open his eyes, yet gives her a warm and welcoming smile and replies "I'm very well, thanks". "Are you ready sir?" She asked him. He replied, "As ready as I'll ever be!". It's a beautiful day with clear skies, sun's rays shining over the calm and perfectly transparent lake surrounded by distant and tall mountains. What a beautiful panoramic view! It seemed like a perfect and happy life, anyone could've dreamed of. Mark's parents walk into the room, both looking depressed and dull. Mrs Twain has tears rolling down her cheeks and Mr Twain is by her side consoling her. She gives Mark a peck on the forehead and a tight hug while he is laying down whispering in his ear "Take care, my darling. I will always love you!" She then walks out of the room without turning her back. Mr

Twain sits next to him with sunken eyes, pecks his forehead and bids him goodbye.

Lisa lives in a quaint town in the English countryside. With no clear direction in her life, the quirky and cheerful young girl moves from job to job to help her tight knit family make ends meet. She knows a lot of things, like how many footsteps there are to the bus stop and that she doesn't love her now boyfriend Sam. It's a warm sunny morning and Lisa is hurriedly walking towards the bus stop. As she gets to work, her manager gives her the bad news that she is no longer needed as he is closing the cafe down. Today will be her last day. "Great!" She thinks back to square one looking for a job.

Lisa calls her friend at the Job Centre, they run through all the options with no luck. At this point Lisa is ready to take anything that comes up as she needs to help her family. Her sister Laura is already working two jobs. An opportunity comes up for a job as a full time carer for a disabled man. The job is to drive, feed and assist. It is a 6 month contract with good money. Her friend convinces her that there are no skills needed and that it's perfect for her and it's not far from home. The people recruiting are very desperate. With a lot of consideration and thought she decides to go for the interview.

During the interview, she makes a lot of obvious mistakes which would make any employer reject her. But to her surprise, she was hired! Mrs Twain liked her chatty, easy going and fast learning character. She was to care for her son, who has quadriplegia, a condition that causes paralysis from the neck down, owing to a car accident two years ago. Lisa happily accepts the job and immediately starts the next day. Confidently and happily she walks into Mark's room and cheerfully introduces herself to him. To her surprise, he is quite cold towards her. This is because of his resentment and bitterness over being disabled. His rudeness doesn't despair her and she continues to learn about the day's activities.

As days pass, the two began to share their experiences together, Mark becomes more communicative and open minded. One day, as Lisa comes to work, she overhears Mark's parents talking about how he attempted to commit suicide as they had turned down his request to end his life at a Swiss based assisted suicide organization. Horrified at his attempt, Mrs Twain promises to honor her son's wish but only if he agrees to live for six months. She believes she will be able to change his mind in the six months and give him a reason to live.

Lisa takes it upon herself to change his life in the six months. She takes him on several outings and places where he would love to go. A deep bond and connection is formed between the two. Mark also learns that his ex-girlfriend is marrying his best friend, which leaves him distraught. Lisa slowly manages to cheer him up and the two end up going for the wedding and having a fabulous time. Mark has never felt this happy since the accident. He reveals to her that she's the only reason why he wakes up in the morning.

Through frequent conversations, Lisa learns that Mark loves reading and has travelled extensively. His favorite place is a café in Paris, where he loves to sit and watch people walk by. Knowing how limited his life is now and the few ambitions he has left, Lisa tries to motivate Mark and make him change. Lisa breaks up with her long term boyfriend Sam because of Mark.

Lisa convinces Mark to go on holiday with her. Just a day before they're due to go, Mark catches pneumonia, which causes them to cancel the trip. Eventually they do end up going on holiday on an island. Both of them are having a magnificent time, being with each other has brought out the best version of each other. One night, Lisa takes Mark for a walk, where they stare into the sky brimming with whirling clouds, shining stars and a yellow crescent moon. Lisa reveals to Mark that she has fallen in love with him. Mark also breaks the news that he is going to the assisted suicide organization in Switzerland to end is life. He can longer bear to be in a wheelchair and be a burden on everyone around him. Upon hearing this Lisa is angry and hurt, and on returning home she quits her job.

Mrs Twain calls her from Switzerland and requests her to come and visit Mark for the last time. Reluctantly she agrees to go. Mark says his final goodbyes to his parents and Lisa. He leaves Lisa an envelope, makes her promise to open it in Paris at his favorite cafe. Lisa learns that Mark has left her an inheritance to complete her studies, which she could not, due to her family's financial difficulties.

Mark wanted to make a contribution to Lisa's life by sacrificing his own life.

What can we learn from this?

Be thankful for what you have and appreciate the little things. The little things are actually big things. We sometimes don't realize how lucky we are until a life-changing event occurs. Life is incredibly precious, anything can change in a moment, cherish what you have now. Everyone has bad days. We forget that there are people who have it much worse than us. Find the blessing in everything around you.

Live boldly and have no regrets. In the simple life that Lisa leads, Mark pushes her to become more proactive. This teaches us there are many opportunities out there and it is up to us to seize it. It's the decisions we take in every moment of our lives that shapes our destiny. Whatever we choose, either good or bad, they are a lesson learned or a blessing. This is what makes us grow.

Lisa knew nothing about the job yet she decided to take it. Had she not decided to take it then her life would be completely different now. Although life throws unexpected days, events or people in our lives, it can turn out for good if you never miss an opportunity. Lisa overcame her fear and brought her dreams to reality. Had Mark not decided to end his life, Lisa's life would be different. She would still be his caregiver and leading a simple life.

Each and every one of us is capable of making a difference. It doesn't matter who we are or what our background is. When you care about someone or something you can change hearts and minds.

Ultimately there are three decisions you make that determine your destiny.

What to focus on?

What things mean to you?

What are you going to do about it?

Can I learn to be more decisive? Yes, it is a skill we can master and practice every day. Whenever you find yourself procrastinating, over-analyzing or authorizing others to make a decision, there are quick and easy steps you can follow.

The power lies in making decisions. Any decision, whether small or big, leads to change which affects us directly and the people around us. It's the fear of change that stops us from being decisive. When you start feeling overwhelmed, or when you feel like you don't have a choice, you can change it all when you decide to do so. Be open to change. Life is always changing and by making a decision even when you are uncertain, you are taking control of it.

Do not overthink a decision. You've made a wrong decision, so what? You learn from it and will learn quickly. It's better than not making any decision at all and remaining stagnant. Make your decision intelligently and quickly and don't ask how or if you can do it. True leadership in business and personal life comes from making decisions; whether they are right or wrong. Stop over analyzing and decide! Life happens for you not to you.

Be committed to your decisions and flexible in your approach. Don't try to be perfect in making decisions. The need to be perfect is another way of fear controlling your decisions. Think of your decisions as learning experiences and the necessity of having to be perfect will fade. Don't be too rigid in your approach, maintain flexibility.

Break the big decision into smaller decisions. Give yourself a time limit on deciding something and taking action. Mastering the skill of making decisions is like strengthening a muscle, and soon enough it gets easier without even thinking about it.

What is it that you're going to choose? Choose wisely!

> "It's in the moments of your decisions that your destiny is shaped"
>
> —Tony Robbins

CHANGE YOUR THOUGHTS... CHANGE YOUR BELIEFS

It's in the wounds where the wisdom lies..

—Oprah

What is a belief? It's an acceptance that something really exists, a strong sense of certainty. For example the sky is blue, is a belief, we never question the validity of this fact.

Beliefs are formed throughout your life and are influenced by the way you were raised and the positive or negative events in your life. These are stories you keep telling yourself using references from experiences. There are two types of beliefs, limiting ones and empowering ones. Limiting beliefs stop you from growing or moving forward in your personal or professional life. Empowering beliefs are beliefs we have about ourselves that are positive and helpful. They increase our capacity to attract our desires.

There is an old story about an elephant and a rope. An old man was passing by an elephant camp when he noticed that the elephants weren't kept in cages or held by chains. All that was holding them back from escaping the camp was a tiny rope tied to their legs. He was very confused as to why the elephants didn't use their strength to break the rope and escape. Curious and wanting an answer, he approached the trainer at the camp. The trainer replied that when they were young and much smaller they used the same rope to tie them, and at that age it was enough to hold them. As they grow older, they were conditioned to believe that the rope holds them so they can never break free. The elephants have adopted a belief that it's just not possible to break free.

The elephants had the belief that it wasn't possible to break free from that tiny rope, so they didn't even try. We all have empowering and disempowering beliefs that are created by certain events or by the way we have been raised. There are limiting beliefs. No matter how much the world tries to hold you back, always continue with the belief that what you want to achieve is always possible. Believing that you can achieve it, is the most important step in achieving it. It is not the environment or the events of our lives but the meaning we attach or how we interpret the situation that makes us who we are today and who we will become tomorrow.

This is a short story about a young nurse who loses her husband abruptly and how she copes with life after his death. There are some meaningful learnings in this story, about how we let our beliefs control our lives.

Sara was a young health worker who lived and worked in a big vibrant lively city. Everything seemed to be perfect for her, she had a kind loving husband, a job that she loved and amazing friends. Sarah had an easy going, happy personality, and everyone who met her instantly liked her. Life was great for her, until the fateful day that changed everything.

Her world was shattered when she lost the love of her life in a car accident. She kept on visiting the events of the tragic day over and over in her head, looking for answers and closure as to why and how something like this could happen. Why did it have to happen to him? What could she have done differently so that he would still be there with her? She became withdrawn and quiet, always kept to herself, even though her friends tried to offer her whatever support they could.

As time went on, she started accepting the reality and slowly opening up to her closest friends. She came across an advertisement in a magazine for a job vacancy for a nurse in a small remote mountain town. She made the decision to take the job, as she felt moving away from the city would help her heal from the tragic death of her husband.

Sara is surprised and startled as she arrives in this beautiful, picturesque town. The cabin looks like nothing she had imagined it to be from the photos that were presented to her. It looked old, dusty and had not been cleaned for a few years! Sara decides to take it upon herself and clean the cabin and make it into a livable place.

Next day she starts her new job, only to be more disappointed. The doctor with whom she is meant to be working with, doesn't really need her help. He is old and set in his ways and thinks he is capable of handling the practice by himself. He immediately rejects her and retaliates towards her. By now, Sara has had enough and considers leaving the town and moving back. The lady, who hired her, convinces her to stay and give it a try. That evening she meets a friendly gentleman, Jack, at the diner; They have a great conversation and both form a bond immediately. He offers to take her around the town, and she agrees. They enjoy each other's company and have a fantastic time together. They spend time together and form a great friendship.

One day Jack reveals how he feels about her, and this takes her aback. She decides to walk away from the friendship and not be in any contact with him. She recalls all the memories of her late husband. Is she comparing her relationship with Jack to her late husband? Has she really healed from the loss?

Sara thought she would move on and heal from the loss once she moved out of town and left all the places and things that reminded her of him. The truth was that she had never really healed from the death. She was looking for external events to help her. Her beliefs had stopped her from forming a friendship and living the life that she wanted. Sara thought and believed that she could never replace her late husband and believed that forming a new relationship was like betraying him. How could she move on and change her perspective and beliefs?

Have you ever felt stuck in a certain area of your life? Do your problems keep on repeating, have you ever felt that despite all your efforts you are not able to achieve anything? For example not being able to lose weight, not being able to grow your income, or always meeting the wrong people in your relationships? In the example of Sara, she was not able to make new friends or have a romantic partner because she had the limiting belief that they would leave her and she would be alone, also that she felt guilty she was betraying her late husband. This is the story she kept telling herself. How do we change a limiting belief to an empowering belief? When you change a limiting belief into an empowering belief, you are tuning your frequency to your desires and hence the attraction happens.

The first thing you have to do is to recognise the story you keep telling yourself. What attractions do you have in that area of your life? What actions are you taking that are supporting this limiting belief? For example, ask yourself, what do I need to believe or think in order to behave this way?

Secondly, we need to break the belief. In order to do this, you need to ask yourself a doubtful question. "Is this 100% true for me? For example for Sara, is it 100% true that she is betraying her late husband? Is this true for everyone, too? By asking these questions it breaks the reference of the belief.

Next step is to anchor the pain to the belief. Associate extreme pain to the limiting belief.

Who do you become if you continue behaving like this? What are the consequences of this behavior?

Lastly, ask yourself. Is it really worth behaving like this? Is it 100% worth experiencing this life? Really feel the emotions you are experiencing.

Now that you have broken the limiting belief, we need to support it with an empowering one. Create an opposite thought or idea. In Sara's story, she created a belief that she is trustworthy and deserving of love.

Ask yourself, is it true? This story alone that you have created is sometimes not enough. It needs to be supported by something around you. By changing her belief that she is worthy and deserving of love, Sara attracted trusting and caring friends. Moving to the new town was a fresh start of her life.

Can you find evidence around you that can support your new story? Ask yourself is this really worth it? Is this worth it for everyone around me, for my family, my friends? Does looking at the evidence make you realize that you need to make changes to your new story?

Supporting your story with facts will help you believe it, but what harbors it into your life is associating it with positive emotions. Visualize whatever is your new story, every detail of it and see how it makes you feel. For example, imagine sitting in a social event, very relaxed and having deep conversations which flow easily between people and see how that makes you feel. Emotion is everything. We all have the capability to imagine. Try it and see what happens.

Beliefs influence your values. If you believe that friendship and connection is the most important thing, your value would be loyalty or trust. When you determine your own values and beliefs and stop making your decision based on what others think, life becomes purposeful.

Our personal values and beliefs deeply affect how we maintain relationships and build new ones. Relationships can cause great joy and happiness sometimes or they can cause intense disappointment and sadness. When you and your partner have conflicting beliefs and values, that relationship is unlikely to last. When there is conflict, drama or arguments in a relationship it means that one person is seeking attention in a negative way. He or she values significance and appreciation more. It is sometimes hard to accept that your values are no longer serving you. Once you recognize this, you can shift yourself into the belief that all relationships are caring and loving. This will strengthen all bonds in relationships. All your values and beliefs are a result of your emotions.

Every thought and action in your day is creating the life you want. Which limiting beliefs are you going to let go of? Make a list of empowering beliefs and disempowering ones. What values support these beliefs? Which ones are you going to let go of? Ask yourself what needs to happen for me to feel a certain emotion.

How do you identify your current belief systems? Recognize your thoughts. Are they positive or negative? Constructive or destructive? Negative and destructive beliefs are formed as a result of opinions and influence of other people. Once you are aware of this, you can change the negative beliefs into empowering beliefs that serve and reflect your true values, not the values of other people.

How do we change a belief?

The most effective way to change a belief is to associate the belief with massive pain- the pain it caused in the past, what it's costing you in the present and what pain it could bring you in the future. Then while adopting a new, empowering belief you must associate great pleasure to it. This pattern should be repeated many times, for it to be embedded into the unconscious mind and to create lasting change. What limiting beliefs are you going to change?

BUILD YOUR LIFE WITH YOUR VALUES

When your values are clear to you, making decisions
becomes easier...

—Roy E Disney

What are the driving forces behind all human behaviour, which impacts our health, relationships, career and money? What are those forces which we are consciously unaware of? What are those forces which is controlling you now and will do so for the rest of your life? The forces are Pain and Pleasure. Everything we do is to either avoid pain or gain pleasure. Our values and beliefs decide what gives us pain and pleasure.

Throughout our lives we have learnt to give labels to different levels of pain and pleasure. These labels are what we call values. Success, determination, motivation, love, security and comfort are all examples of values. If you were asked to pick one, which one would you choose? One person may pick success while another one will go for love, etc. All of us have learnt to take different words we call emotions, and give them different levels of importance and different levels of intensity. All the above emotions are pleasurable, but we don't feel them at the same time. We don't value all these states at the same level. What are values? Values are standards that we set for ourselves for what is good, meaningful and fair. Our values are things we fundamentally want to move towards. If we don't, we don't feel whole and fulfilled. They also determine what we move away from. They control our lifestyle.

How can we use this understanding to alter our lives?

In our daily lives, we only pay attention to a small band of our experiences and the rest is deleted from our brain. What we pay attention to, what we focus on is based on our values. Our values tell us what emotion we should focus on because they will lead us to lots of pleasure. We also have some values that we pay attention to, but are painful and we want to avoid them at any cost. We call these two types of values as moving towards values and moving away values. Examples of moving towards values are happiness, security, love, success, comfort and certainty. They create pleasure. Examples of moving away values include frustration, depression, anger, physical pain, humiliation, sadness. We move away from these to avoid pain. From all these states which one would you avoid the most? We try to avoid all of them but the way we organise them according to their importance is called hierarchy of values. Our brain does whatever it can, to avoid painful experiences and does almost anything it can, to gain pleasure.

Let's take an example of an opportunity when I got to go skydiving in my mid twenties.

A small aeroplane took off, without the door being closed. I happened to be sitting right next to it and on my left was my instructor. I looked at him anxiously and sceptically, and all he did was to give me a huge smile. I was really scared and nervous. But something inside me told me to do it anyway. As the aeroplane reached a certain altitude, my instructor finally closed the door. I felt at ease and calmer. Finally, we had reached an altitude of 12,000 feet and it was time to take the plunge. He opened the door, I sat at the edge of the plane, with my instructor behind me. My heart started beating faster and I felt a rush of adrenaline. The wind rushed on my face and before I knew it we were floating in the sky among the clouds. I felt safe as I knew my instructor was on my back. Being up in the clouds was so peaceful. A few seconds later, the parachute opened and we were flying down. Everything from the top appeared so minute and my breath was taken away. We slowly came down to earth.

How did my brain decide that this experience is going to lead to pain or pleasure? It considers what is important in my life, considers all kinds of acknowledgement and rewards of being adventurous, outrageous and playful. I had some previous experiences where I was so afraid of doing something adventurous, but after doing it I felt so incredible. My brain made that neuro-association that adventure is total pleasure. This means that adventure, outrageousness are likely to be high on my list. On the contrary, if I had security as my highest value, I would not do anything that could cause physical pain or fear. It is very unlikely that I would go skydiving, as it's linked to pain and fear.

Where do these values come from? They come from the environment you are in, starting from when you were a baby. Your parents also had a major role, telling you what they did or did not, what they want you to do or say or believe. If you accepted them you were rewarded, if you rejected them you were punished. As you got older your values came from another source, your peer groups. When you first started playing with them, they had a different set of values from yours. You blended your values with theirs or altered your own so that you don't get bullied or neglected by others. Throughout your life you are constantly creating new peer groups where you are blending your values with theirs or altering your own. Our values are the ultimate key to understand and predict our own behaviour as well as the behaviour of others.

What is the one thing all leaders like Steve Jobs, Warren Buffet, Mother Teresa have in common? It is their power. It is their own power that has led them to success, to build relationships, to stand out from the crowd. What is the definition of power? It is the capacity to access your internal resources and use them towards creating your desires and achieving them. We are all born with power resources and weak resources. Power resources help you gain power to achieve your goals, while weak resources make us powerless. That is why we are held back sometimes, even when we want to produce results. Examples of power resources are staying focused, being motivated, being honest and sincere, and being creative. On the other hand, examples of weak resources are; procrastination, laziness, demotivation, etc. Leaders are powerful because they know and have the ability to access their internal resources. Ordinary people are unable to do this consciously, hence they sometimes feel powerless. Where does the source of power come from? It comes from our values. We are most powerful when we are working towards our highest values. We automatically become powerful and gain access to our internal resources. On the contrary, when we work with our lowest values we become powerless, and hence become lazy, demotivated, careless, etc.

It is our values that determine whether we have the drive to take action or sit back, whether we are able to cooperate with people or not, whether we will fail or succeed. When we are clear about what our values are, we can easily access our internal resources to take action towards our desires. How do you determine what your highest values are? We have different values for our work, relationships and family. To identify this, ask yourself; what is most important to me in my relationships? For example, if it is support, again ask the question what is important about support? It could be that someone loves you. Continue asking the question until you get a list of values. Below is an example of a list of values for life:

Energetic

Passionate

Love

Significant

Growth

Contribution

Happiness

Excitement

Joy

Ecstasy

While you are asking the question of what is more important to you, something may come up. You may say buying a house is more important to me, or money is more important to me. These are just processes, what we actually want is the feeling when buying a house. What feeling does buying a house can provide you? Perhaps a sense of security, stability and belongingness. There are two types of values: Process/ material values and emotional/ end values. Buying a house is a process value and the emotion you get from buying the house is the end value. We want the end value not the process.

Our brain will do more to avoid pain than to gain pleasure. We also need to make a list of away values, emotions or states that you do most to avoid. Below is an example:

Frustration

Hurt

Anger

Humiliation

Disappointment

Embarrassment

Why do you want to find out what your values are? Because you want to find out what your brain is most focused on, and by changing your values you change your destiny. Our values are constantly changing at every stage of our lives. The key is the awareness of the change.

Even if you don't change your values, there is something you must do to take control of your destiny and your life; that is to understand the power of your beliefs to impact the quality of your life. Your beliefs and values work together to determine how you feel. For example if your value is to be successful, what has to happen for you to be successful? This is a rule that you set for yourself in order for you to have this value.

Rules are conditioned beliefs. We may have the same values but different rules for the values to be met. For example, one person may have a rule that if they make enough money then they're successful and another person may have a rule that people will like me only when I'm successful. We unconsciously create easy rules for feeling negative and difficult rules for feeling positive. In order to change, we must make easy rules to feel positive and difficult rules to feel negative.

By determining the rules a person lives by, it's easy to predict their behaviour and needs. What rules are you going to create? Be sure to create easy, empowering rules for your values that will create your ultimate destiny and dream life!

UNDERSTAND PEOPLE THROUGH 6 HUMAN NEEDS

Success is liking yourself, liking what you do and liking how you do it.....

—Maya Angelou

Why do we do what we do? Why do people crave love? Why do people take drugs? Why do people overeat or overspend? Everybody has a reason as to why they do what they do, whether they are aware of it or not. What does it take to be successful? You could have a lot of money yet not be happy. Many people think that being successful is being rich. If you are rich and not fulfilled, you have failed. Success without fulfillment is failure. How do you make sure you are fulfilled? We all have six needs that must be met, all human beings do.

The first need we all have is the need for comfort or certainty. This is a survival need, we all need to feel certain that we can avoid pain and have comfort. For some people this is their highest need. If anything changes in their life, they become fearful, freak out or they get angry. What matters to them is keeping things the same way and thus being in control of the situation. Every single person has their own way of meeting that basic need. The question is, are you meeting this need in a way that is empowering you or disempowering you?

The second need is the need for change. We don't only crave certainty but also change. What if you could already know what is going to happen at every moment of the day? What if you could predict what a particular person is going to say? You would be bored of your life - hence the need for uncertainty, variety and surprises. Change creates excitement for us. It makes us alive. We can make changes by having new goals, learning new things, having a conversation with a friend, setting up a challenge and so on. Just like the need for certainty, we all strive to meet the need for change in ways that are positive, negative or neutral.

The third human need is importance - the need to feel that our lives are significant, unique and special. There are many ways to feel special, like working hard to achieve something, finding your uniqueness by giving more than anyone else, dressing uniquely, knowing more about sports than anyone else you know. There are also negative ways of feeling important like violence and theft. Violence is the cheapest and fastest way to get the feeling of importance from others. What are your ways of feeling important?

The fourth one is love and connection. Just as the need for comfort reveals the need for change, the need for feeling important reveals the need for love and connection. The answer to the question why people do what they do has always been love.

People find connection through friendships, sports, community, pets, art and meditation. We can experience connection even through illness, when someone looks after us. Another way is by creating problems. A good example of this is a child throwing a tantrum because you did not give him enough attention. Adults do it in a more dramatic way, like pleasing people all the time just to get the connection or resorting to illegal behaviour. Most people settle for connection because love is too scary, they don't want to get hurt and have their hearts broken. True love is absolute joy, comfort and passion.

The final two needs are growth and contribution. These needs create fulfillment and are spiritual needs. The first four needs are the basic needs for our personality. Everyone does everything to meet the first four needs. We either grow or die. If our relationship is not growing it's dying. If our business is not growing it's dying. Growth is life. Anytime you start changing some aspect of your life you are making progress and that's what brings happiness.

Contribution is the need to step out of ourselves, it is the need for service. When we give, we live in a world of abundance and compassion. When something good happens we immediately want to share it with the people we love. Why? There is only so much pleasure we can feel internally, and by sharing, it multiplies.

We all have different goals and desires but we have the same needs. We all behave differently despite having the same six needs. This is because we value them differently. All human beings prioritise these needs differently, but you have the power to choose what to focus on. Some people may have love and connection as their top most need, others may have significance and another person may choose certainty. Most people meet their needs in a way that feels good in the short term and not long term. This could be by over eating, smoking, taking drugs, etc. People will give up their goals and dreams to meet their needs.

Anytime your brain perceives that doing something, believing something or feeling something meets three of your needs then you will become addicted to that thought, that feeling, that emotion or that action. This could be positive, negative or neutral.

Why do we do what we do?

Understanding the six human needs and how they can affect your decisions, you can easily identify and correct the negative effects of them in your life. You can make empowering positive shifts and change the direction of your life. The sequence of the needs creates the frequency and hence the attraction.

CREATE A
COMPELLING
FUTURE!

With everything that has happened to you, you
can either feel sorry for yourself or treat what
has happened as a gift. Everything is either an
opportunity to grow or an obstacle to keep you from
growing. You get to choose.

—Wayne Dyer

We've all experienced pain at different
levels, and in different forms. It's our
choice what we decide to do with it, either
dwell in the negative space, or choose to see the
positive side and the goodness it has created.
Life is a balance, for every negative there is
always a positive. This is the grand plan of the
universe. If we blame someone for the pain
they caused us, we may as well acknowledge
them for the goodness they brought to the

situation. We all need change in order to grow. Most of us wait until something happens before we finally decide to make a shift. Changes are created in a moment.

Most people believe that change takes a long time. Why? This is because they have tried again and again to make the change through their will power but failed. They have also made the assumption that the most important changes take a long time and are very difficult to make. We make it difficult for ourselves because we don't know how to change and don't have an effective strategy for it. If we want to make long lasting change, will power alone is not enough.

Another reason as to why change doesn't happen quickly is because we have a set of beliefs that prevent us from using our truest and inner most potential. For many people, quick change would mean that you don't have a problem in your current situations. For example, how long would you grieve the death of a loved one? Practically, the intense grief will last for the next few days and you will recover from it. But most of us tend to grieve for a much longer period. Why? Because we have a set of beliefs in our culture that you need to grieve for a certain amount of time and if you don't, you didn't love that person enough. They have linked pain to grieving. While in other cultures they celebrate life after the death of a loved one, because they believe that there is always a right time for us to leave this earth. If you grieve, it is believed that you have a lack of understanding of life and that you are selfish. They link pleasure to death and pain to grieving. It is our beliefs that make our pain difficult to recover from.

We have all heard the saying that everything is energy. Once you have a clear understanding that everything is energy, you open the door to shaping your world into anything you want. Universal energy is what makes up matter which in turn is a building block of everything we encounter. According to the work of Albert Einstein, energy can neither be created nor destroyed, and no further energy can be created- there is enough for everyone. Energy is always vibrating at a frequency and frequency creates state. If the frequency changes, then the state changes. Frequency can change your life.

The frequency we vibrate at is made up of our feelings, thoughts, beliefs and actions. Our emotions are made up of energy. Different emotions carry different energy and hence different frequencies. For example happiness has a specific frequency, so does jealousy. Thoughts have vibrations - positive and negative frequencies. Negative thoughts match the negative frequency and you start attracting negative things, situations and bad luck. When you are in a positive state of mind, you influence all energy around you in a positive way. How do you change frequency?

We all have emotional patterns. We feel certain emotions at certain times of the day. This is what we call our habitual and comfortable emotional home. These unique patterns or habits have an intense influence on the way we perceive things in life, the way we behave and how good we are at moving on from the past. Our emotions are like a muscle that we can train. We can train ourselves to feel frustrated, angry and sad when a difficult situation arises or we can train ourselves to feel strong, calm and passionate in the same situation. How do we take charge of our emotions?

Many of us think that emotions simply happen to us, but in fact emotions are a result of our physical and mental states which is determined by our body physiology and what we focus on. For example, if you are sitting with your shoulders dropped and your head lowered, and you choose to focus on thoughts that are negative, you will naturally feel depressed and upset. By having your head up high and shoulders straight, you will naturally feel calmer and happier. By choosing to focus on the positive aspects of the situation rather than the negative, you will feel lighter and freer. By also changing how we see, feel and what we hear in the situation, we can change the focus. Giving a positive meaning or no meaning to the situation will also help in shifting the emotional habits to empowering ones. Taking these steps to change your emotional patterns will in turn change your energy and hence improve the frequency you're vibrating at, to make better attractions in your life. Keep a record of how you feel from the time you wake up to the time you go to bed for a week. You will notice at which times of the day you feel certain emotions and then use the techniques described above to change it.

Below is a true story which outlines the courage and beliefs of a young girl.

A beautiful girl was born to a young couple. Pregnancy is a joyous occasion but not to them, as they were young and unmarried and in the earlier days it was considered shameful. The couple separated and the little girl was sent to be raised by her grandmother, while her mother travelled north to find a home and secure a job.

Her grandmother taught her how to read in her early years and took her to church where she would read the passages out aloud. At the age of 5, she started kindergarten and very quickly was moved to grade 1 when they saw how quickly she could read and write.

Unfortunately the girl's grandmother fell sick. She was then sent to live with her mother and half sister. A year later she went to live with her dad and stepmother where she settled in well. She was moved to third grade and she got involved with the church, too, and started public speaking. She went to visit her mother and half sister during the summer holidays and decided to stay with her mother. She was 9 years old then. While babysitting her siblings, she was raped by her nineteen year old cousin. This was her first experience of sexual abuse. As time went on, her family members would continually assault her until one day she fell pregnant. This became traumatizing for her and she kept it all to herself. She began skipping school and stealing which was too much for her mother to handle. She found out her teenage daughter was pregnant and sent her to live with her father as the detention homes were full. The girl was at a rock bottom and actually considered committing suicide.

Her father provided her with a safe and loving home. She gave birth to a baby boy who died two weeks later due to complications of being born prematurely. It was her father's support that gave her courage to move forward and leave the painful past behind. She then landed a job in the local radio while still in high school and by the age of 19, she was the co- anchor for the local evening news. Her emotional delivery eventually led her to transfer to the daytime talk show arena. She boosted it from a third-rated talk show to first place. She then opened her own production company.

This girl is no one but Oprah Winfrey. She trusted her own instincts and followed her passions to the public eye. She didn't know how but just followed her strong instincts. This is her story from rags to riches. She's reinvented her show with a focus on self improvement, mindfulness and spirituality. Oprah is best known for her talk show, she was the richest African American of the 20th century and the world's only black billionaire.

Oprah believes that her incredible hardship experiences have made her successful. The loneliness that she suffered as a young child has taught her to be more independent and fend for herself as she was all she had. She also learned that happiness is something you find internally and not something you search for in others. She believes that having determination and an open mind is what turns your struggles into strengths. It is her beliefs and experiences from childhood that have made her the person she is. She's used her pain to change her beliefs.

It's not the environment nor the events that happened in Oprah's life but the meaning she gave it and how she interpreted that event made her become who she is today. Taking the lessons from Oprah's story, what are you going to change in your life? How are you going to make that change?

Creating empowering rituals can also contribute to make that big change in your life. Changing little things like having a healthy breakfast, taking 20 minutes to meditate every day, walking and exercising and learning a new skill will lead to consistency and massive change. It's the little things that make the big difference in life.

Being grateful for what you have rather than thinking what you don't have will also create empowering emotions. Practicing gratitude everyday is another meaningful and powerful way to change emotions. Be present in the moment rather than worry about the past or future. Enjoy the moment as it is.

Everyone has a different life journey. We are all here to learn different lessons at different times of our lives. This is what makes us special and unique. It's not our experiences that are good or bad, but our perceptions of them. Our worst experiences can teach us the greatest lessons, and take us through the destiny of life.

Have the courage to turn your dreams into reality, follow your intuition. One of the greatest powers we possess is the power to shift your perceptions. You can truly change your life and of those around you by becoming aware of your perceptions. As the author of your life, you can change your story by changing your perceptions. Change what you focus on and what meaning you give to any situation. Decide what you want and believe that no challenge, no obstacle or problem can keep you from it. You can take control of your life the moment you decide that your life is not shaped by your conditions but by your decisions. Make your beliefs and values empowering to shape life on your terms. Find ways of meeting your needs in a positive and resourceful way, create your reality.

The universe has given us the gift of life.. How do you want to be remembered? Live your life fully, and in the moment. Experience everything in life, have fun, do crazy things, make mistakes, take all opportunities to learn from them. Find the root cause of your problems and eliminate them. Don't try to be perfect, just be human!

Life is happening for you, not to you!